OCTOPUS' DEN

SMITHSONIAN OCEANIC COLLECTION

For my mother, who taught me that some things
aren't just icky, squishy, and strange — they're also fascinating.
   — D.L.

To Rita Edwards, for her love and enthusiastic support.
   — S.J.P.

Book Design: Shields & Partners, Westport, CT

First Edition 1997
10 9 8 7 6 5 4 3 2
Printed in China

Acknowledgements:
   Soundprints wishes to thank Dr. Clyde F. E. Roper of the Department of Invertebrate Zoology at the
Smithsonian's National Museum of Natural History for his curatorial review.
   Steven James Petruccio wishes to thank Peg Siebert and Blodgett Memorial Library for their research assistance;
Schuyler M. Bull, Lisa Prial, Cassia Farkas, and Diane Hinze Kanzler for all their efforts; his family for their patience
and support; and Bud and Evelyne Johnson for being there.

Library of Congress Cataloging-in-Publication Data

Langeland, Deirdre. 1973-

Octopus' den / by Deirdre Langeland; illustrated by Steven Petruccio.
         p.   cm.
Summary: Octopus encounters danger as he returns to his den, finds it claimed by another of his kind, and
ventures out to seek a new home.
         ISBN 1-56899-473-7
1. Octopus — Juvenile Fiction. [1. Octopus — Fiction.]
I. Petruccio, Steven, ill. II. Title.
         PZ10.3.L345Oc   1997
         [Fic] — dc21   97-8676
                                                          CIP
                                                          AC

OCTOPUS' DEN

by Deirdre Langeland   Illustrated by Steven James Petruccio

Soundprints
Where Children Discover...

Twenty feet below the blue surface of the Mediterranean
Sea, the sandy sea floor lies in folds and ripples. Fan
mussels and sea grass grow on patches of gravel nestled between
tiny sand hills. One sand hill is different from the others. It has two
bright eyes peeking out from it — one to the right, one to the left.
Cleverly disguised, Octopus is waiting for his dinner.

Before long a crab creeps by. It moves sideways, tall on its hard-shelled legs. Close, close, closer. Suddenly, one of Octopus' long arms shoots out and the crab is caught. Try as it might, it cannot break free from Octopus' strong suction cups.

Octopus uses his sharp beak to break open the crab's shell and eat his slippery meal.

It has been a long night of hunting for Octopus, and it is time for him to return to his den.

But his round eyes spot something interesting in the distance. From a tangle of seaweed, half buried by sand, a shiny piece of glass reflects the morning sunlight. Slowly, carefully, Octopus crawls toward the strange object.

With a flash, the sun glints off its bright surface. Curious, Octopus creeps closer and slithers behind a nearby rock.

For a moment the sea floor is quiet. Then, slowly, Octopus' eyes stretch up from behind the rock like periscopes. From his hiding place, Octopus watches the seaweed for signs of danger.

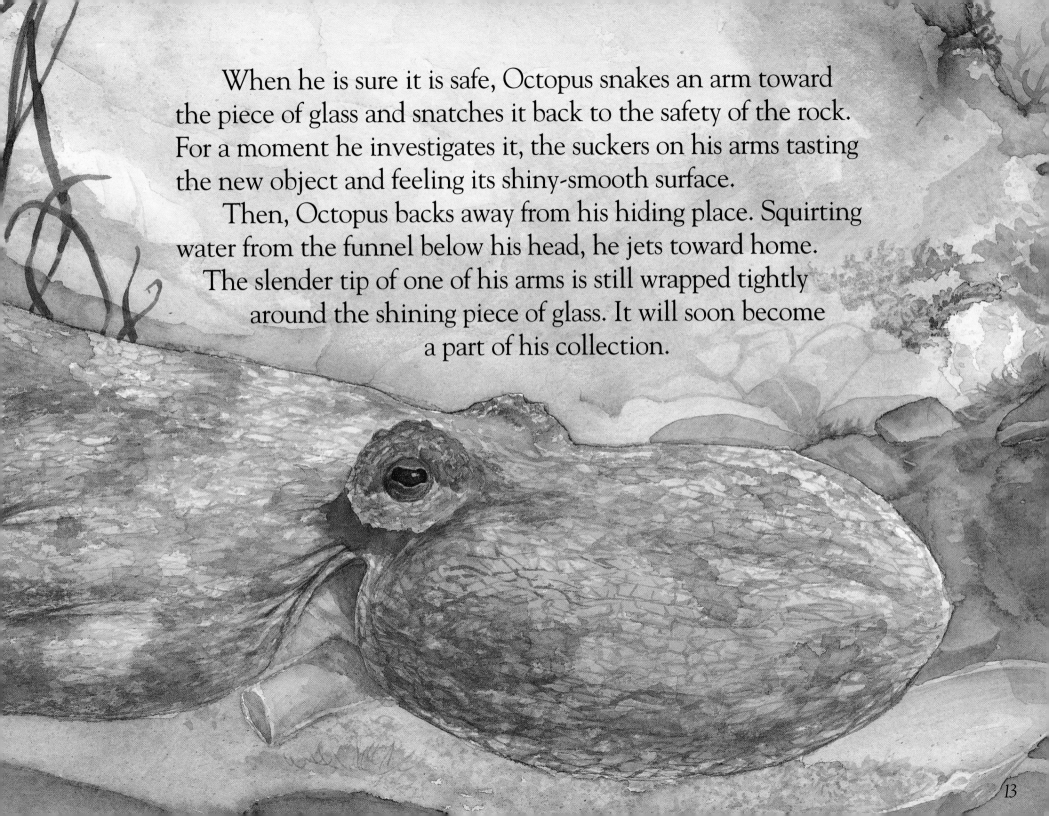

When he is sure it is safe, Octopus snakes an arm toward the piece of glass and snatches it back to the safety of the rock. For a moment he investigates it, the suckers on his arms tasting the new object and feeling its shiny-smooth surface.

Then, Octopus backs away from his hiding place. Squirting water from the funnel below his head, he jets toward home. The slender tip of one of his arms is still wrapped tightly around the shining piece of glass. It will soon become a part of his collection.

But before he reaches his safe den, Octopus spies danger. From between two rocks, a hungry moray eel prepares to strike. Its smooth, thin body is wedged tightly in the rocks, where few other creatures can fit. It is ready to attack with lightning speed.

Octopus acts swiftly. His body turns dark and he squirts a cloud of ink at the eel. The ink hangs in the water like another shadowy octopus.

The eel attacks the cloud. It doesn't see Octopus shoot off in the opposite direction. Octopus changes color again, this time to a sandy shade of gray and rockets behind a stony outcropping.

The eel is confused by the ink. It cannot smell Octopus. It bursts through the cloud and glides right over him.

As the eel disappears into the distance, Octopus stretches out his body, and begins to rise toward a hole in a rocky undersea cliff — his home.

Just as he is about to slide into the hidden rock-hole, he sees that something else is there. A larger octopus has moved in. The big octopus is wedged tightly into the hole, sitting on shells and rocks that Octopus collected.

The intruder reaches a huge arm toward Octopus, the suckers facing out, warning him to stay away. Octopus obeys. He will have to find a new home.

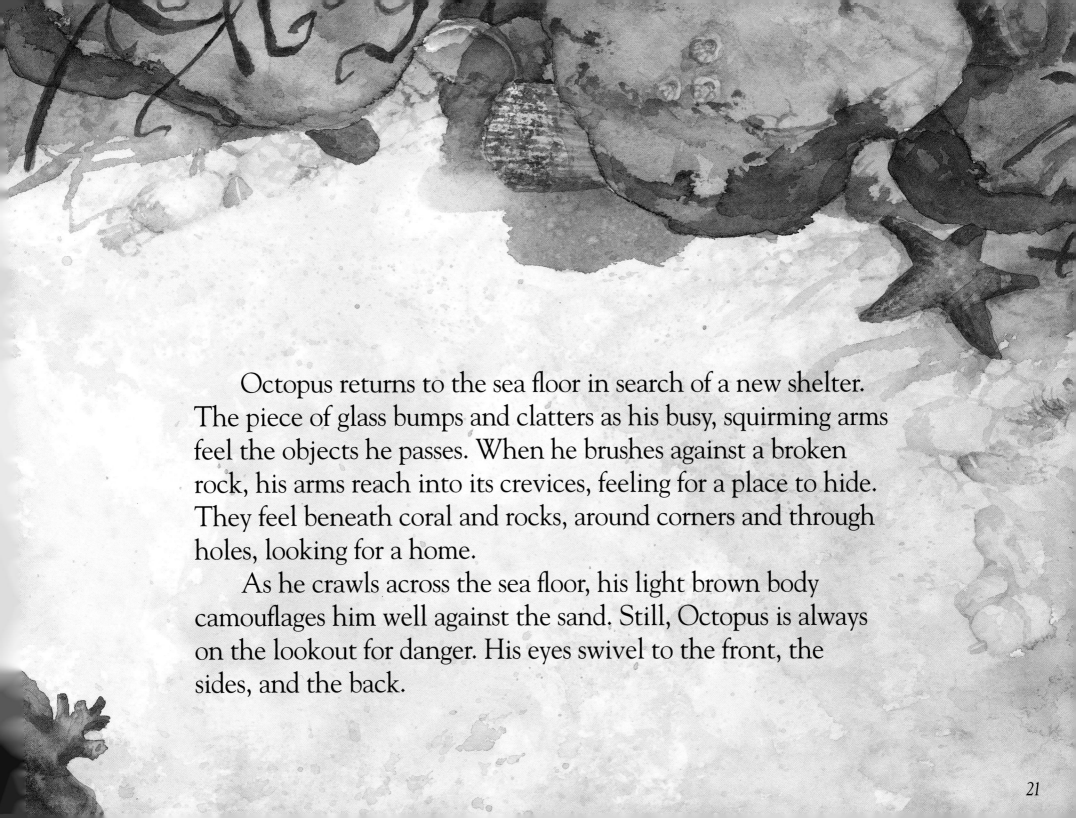

Octopus returns to the sea floor in search of a new shelter. The piece of glass bumps and clatters as his busy, squirming arms feel the objects he passes. When he brushes against a broken rock, his arms reach into its crevices, feeling for a place to hide. They feel beneath coral and rocks, around corners and through holes, looking for a home.

As he crawls across the sea floor, his light brown body camouflages him well against the sand. Still, Octopus is always on the lookout for danger. His eyes swivel to the front, the sides, and the back.

The sun's rays are growing dim when Octopus reaches a rocky shelf. Here, gentle afternoon sunlight streaks down from the sky, bathing the sea floor in a green glow. A school of silvery fish weaves between dark coral branches. Octopus reaches around the coral. There is no home there.

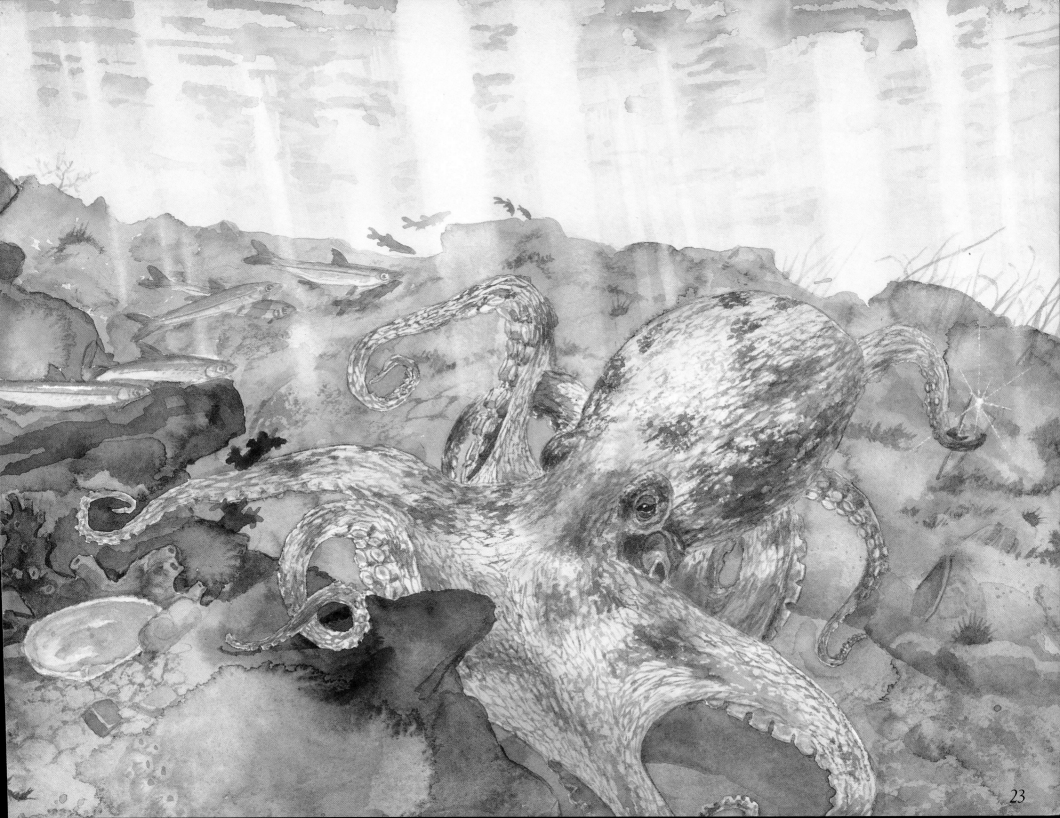

Nearby, a sea horse floats in the still water, its tail twisted around a stalk of green seaweed. Octopus moves past it. One arm brushes the seaweed, jiggling the seahorse around.
Another arm reaches over a huge gray rock.
A third snakes around it.
There, hidden beneath the giant rock, Octopus discovers a hiding place.

The tiny opening is the size of an apple.
Octopus pours his body through it and explores
the cave beneath. It is just the right size —
too small for an eel or grouper, but perfect for a
flexible octopus. Satisfied that he has found a safe shelter,
Octopus begins his house cleaning.

Octopus squirts water from his funnel, blowing pebbles and
shells out the tiny doorway. Sand rises in a murky cloud until the
den is clear, ready for Octopus to move in.

Next, Octopus builds a fence. With his front arms, he sweeps gravel away from the hole to make a little clearing. Then he gathers materials and cleans them. Pieces of rock, jagged and smooth, empty clam shells, broken coral, and the sparkling piece of glass — all become part of a fence for Octopus.

Finally, Octopus' home is complete. As night comes, he slips inside.

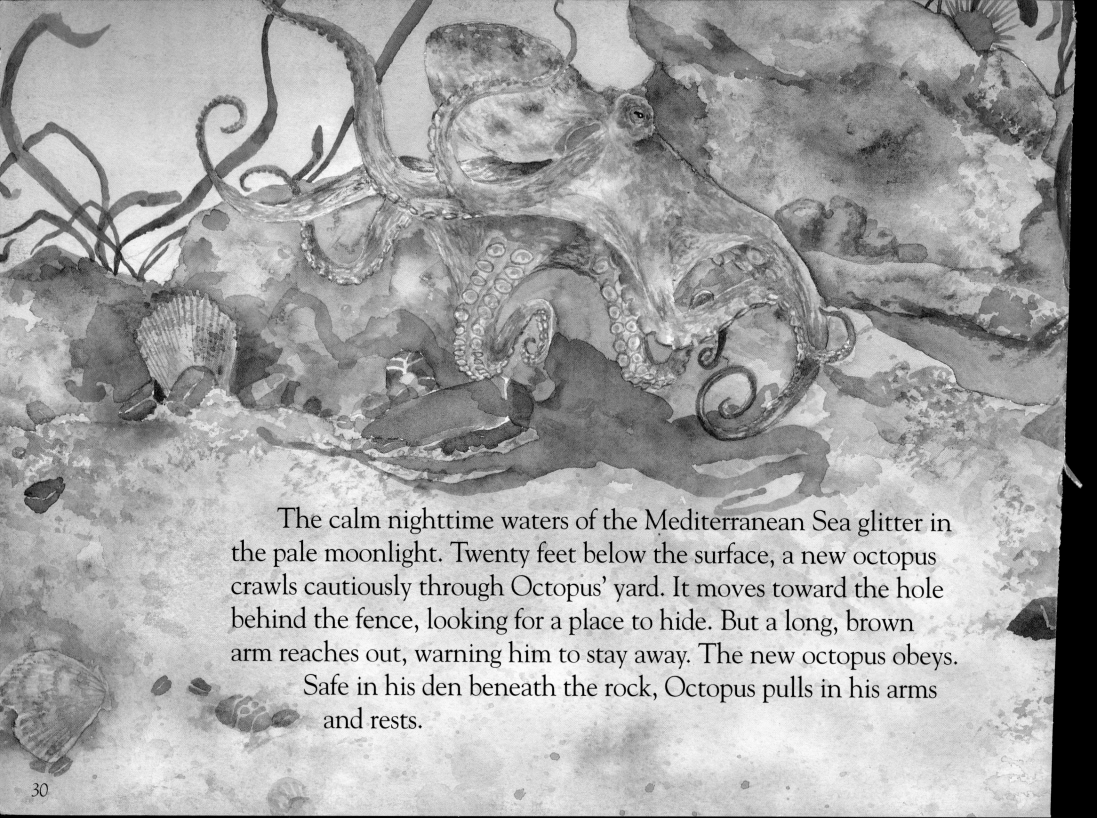

The calm nighttime waters of the Mediterranean Sea glitter in the pale moonlight. Twenty feet below the surface, a new octopus crawls cautiously through Octopus' yard. It moves toward the hole behind the fence, looking for a place to hide. But a long, brown arm reaches out, warning him to stay away. The new octopus obeys. Safe in his den beneath the rock, Octopus pulls in his arms and rests.